THE RUBBISH SUPER EXPERT SCIENCE QUIZ

THE RUPA BOOK OF SUPER EXPERT SCIENCE QUIZ

Dilip M. Salwi

Rupa & Co

*In memory of
the Late P.R. Tawde*

Copyright © Dilip M. Salwi 2004

First Published 2004
Fourth Impression 2011

Published by
Rupa Publications India Pvt. Ltd.
7/16, Ansari Road, Daryaganj,
New Delhi 110 002

Sales Centres:

Allahabad Bengaluru Chennai
Hyderabad Jaipur Kathmandu
Kolkata Mumbai

Printed in India by
Gopsons Papers Ltd.
A-14 Sector 60
Noida 201 301

Hello! Science Quiz Buffs!

More than fifteen years ago, when my publisher suggested I write a science quiz book, I was somewhat reluctant. I had written quiz questions on science for a children's magazine from my college days and so I thought I should do something different. But his persuasion finally won me over, and I sat down to write the book.

At the outset I decided that my book would, despite being a quiz book, give a holistic, total picture of science and technology, including the effects of science on society. In consultation with my friend Dr. N.R. Mankad I thought of having 1000 quiz questions in the book with the hope that it would turn out to be the magical number. And so it has. Published in 1988, it has today gone into more than 18 editions and is still the best-selling quiz book. Subsequently, my publisher brought out a 1000 series of quiz books on other subject. In due couse, some clones of my book also appeared in the market. Who says students are not interested in science?

Naturally, such an old quiz book needs revision and updating as the scientific scenario has changed over the years. I have also split the aforementioned book into two handy parts with more new questions but retaining the holistic flavour of the previous book. In tune with the popular 'Super Quiz' series I brought out recently for kids and children, I have also renamed the two books, 'Super Expert Science Quiz' and 'Super Genius Science

Quiz'. For easy reading of the answers, I have also changed the format. I have also included a scoring board to assess oneself in science awareness. I am sure all these changes will be appreciated by my young readers.

I reiterate here that these books test your 'Science Awareness' and not science as such becasue it is my personal feeling that science cannot be tested by quiz questions. I am sure they will prove as attractive and stimulating to my young readers as the previous book proved to be. If these books sustain my readers' interest in science and technology in these days when it is present in all walks of life, my purpose in writing them will be fulfilled.

Delhi
July 19, 2003

Dilip M. Salwi

Acknowledgements

The following agencies and individuals are to be thanked for the photographs published in the book: Asoka Samanta, U.S.I.S., New Delhi; Ravi Datta, British High Commission, New Delhi; Shankar, French Information Center, New Delhi; German News Agency, New Delhi; Indian Space Research Organisation, Bangalore; Raman Research Institute, Bangalore; World Health Organisation, New Delhi; Bose Institue, Kolkata; Visvesvaraya Industrial Museum of Science and Technology, Bangalore; Dinesh Sinha and P.Dayanandan. And last but not the least, I am thankful to Ajay Gupta for keying the book on the computer and my wife Smriti, daughter Neha and son Romel for bearing patiently with me while I was revising this book.

Dilip M. Salwi

CONTENTS

I

FIRST THINGS FIRST

First Scientists

1. Who was the first to operate a computer using computer language?
   - (a) George Stibitz
   - (b) Charles Babbage
   - (c) G. W. Leibniz
   - (d) Konard Zuse

2. Who was the first to use the symbols ♂ and ♀ for male and female?
   - (a) Aristotle
   - (b) Charles Darwin
   - (c) Carolus Linnaeus
   - (d) Richard Owen

3. Who built the first cyclotron machine to accelerate electric particles to high energies?
   - (a) Enrico Fermi
   - (b) E. O. Lawrence
   - (c) Alexendro Volta
   - (d) Robert J. Van de Graff

4. Who was the first to invent the technique of producing test tube babies?
   (a) Patrick Steptoe   (b) Robert Edwards
   (c) None   (d) Both

5. Who was the first to observe the atmosphere of the planet Venus?
   (a) Mikhail Lomonosov   (b) George Airy
   (c) Giovanni Cassini   (d) Francis Baily

6. Who built the first nuclear reactor, the 'Atomic pile'?
   (a) Otto Hahn   (b) H. J. Bhabha
   (c) Freeman Dyson   (d) Enrico Fermi

7. Who first gave the concept of 'atom'?
   (a) Kanada   (b) Aristotle
   (c) John Dalton   (d) Kapila

8. Who was the first to determine the size of the earth correctly?
   (a) Ptolemy   (b) Hipparchus
   (c) Eratosthenes   (d) Archimedes

9. Who was the first person to drill out oil from beneath the surface of the earth?
   (a) John Dalton   (b) Edwin Drake
   (c) Alfred Wegener   (d) Justus von Liebig

10. Who was the first to build ar electron microscope?
    (a) Max Knoll and Ernst Ruska
    (b) Anton van Leeuwenhoek
    (c) H. Binnig   (d) Robert Millikan

11. Who claimed for the first time that the earth is a sphere and it rotates around its axis?
    (a) Aryabhata   (b) Varahamihira
    (c) Pythagoras   (d) Ptolemy

12. Who was the first to design and build the pedal-powered aircraft that flew?
    (a) Henry Kremer   (b) Bryan Allen
    (c) Paul MacCready   (d) Charles Lindbergh

13. Who was the first hang-glider pilot?
    (a) Otto Lilienthal   (b) James Van Allen
    (c) Orville Wright   (d) William Lassell

14. Who first treated zero as a number and showed its mathematical operations?
    (a) Brahmagupta   (b) Aryabhata
    (c) Plato   (d) Pythagoras

15. Who was the first to detect radio waves?
    (a) G. Macroni   (b) James C. Maxwell
    (c) Heinrich Hertz   (d) Nicola Tesla

16. Who was the first to show that Ice Ages had once invaded the earth?
    - (a) Gabrial Daubree
    - (b) George Cuvier
    - (c) Charles Lyell
    - (d) Louis Agassiz

17. Who was the first to work out the principles of rocketry?
    - (a) Robert Goddard
    - (b) Hermann Oberth
    - (c) Willy Ley
    - (d) Konstantin Tsiolkovsky

18. Who first showed that something divided by zero is an infinite quantity?
    - (a) Brahmagupta
    - (b) Bhaskara
    - (c) Leonardo da Vinci
    - (d) Mahavira

19. Who first thought of the invention of computer in totality?
    - (a) Al-Kashi
    - (b) G. W. Leibniz
    - (c) Charles Babbage
    - (d) Countess Lovelace

20. Who was the first to discover a new planet?
    - (a) William Herschel
    - (b) William Lassell
    - (c) John Herschel
    - (d) Urbain Leverrier

21. Who first detected the phenomenon of hot super conductivity?
    (a) Johannes Georg Bednorz
    (b) Karl Alex Muller
    (c) Walter Meissner
    (d) Heike Kamerlingh-Onnes

First Things

22. Which was the first computer language?
    (a) FORTRAN   (b) PLANKALKUEL
    (c) BABBAGE   (d) PL-1

23. Which tree was the first to be cultivated as a crop?
    (a) Haldu   (b) Lac tree
    (c) Peepal   (d) Date palm

24. Which was the first molecule to be discovered in space?
    (a) Carbon dioxide
    (b) Carbon monoxide
    (c) Silicon oxide   (d) Hydroxide

25. Who sent the first e-mail to his friend?
    (a) Larry Roberts   (b) Ray Tomlinson
    (c) William Gates   (d) Robert Kahn

26. Which is the first computer that appeared to be intelligent?
    (a) Eliza
    (b) Intel
    (c) EDVAC
    (d) Cyber

27. Who built the first scientific laboratory in the true sense of the term?
    (a) Lord Kelvin
    (b) Jean Focault
    (c) Louis Pasteur
    (d) Jean Agassiz

28. Which is the first element to be transmuted into another by means of high energy machines 'Accelerators' ?
    (a) Plutonium
    (b) Helium
    (c) Gold
    (d) Lithium

29. Who discovered the first 'Homo erectus' fossil – the Java Ape man?
    (a) Eugene Dubois
    (b) Raymond Dart
    (c) Mary Leakey
    (d) Tim White

30. Who is believed to have built the first chain of astronomical observatories in the world?
    (a) Varahamihira
    (b) Aryabhata
    (c) M. N. Saha
    (d) Sawai Jai Singh II

31. Which is the first weather satellite?
    (a) Meteor-I
    (b) Tiros-I
    (c) Bhaskara-I
    (d) Meteosat

32. What is the name of the first test-tube baby?
    (a) Louise Brown
    (b) Juliet Edwards
    (c) Lesley Brown
    (d) Alistair Montgomery

33. Where was the first modern astronomical observatory built in India?
    (a) Naini Tal
    (b) Hyderabad
    (c) Chennai
    (d) Kolkata

34. Which is the first wholly synthetic fibre?
    (a) Rayon
    (b) Wool
    (c) Nylon
    (d) Teflon

35. Which is the first invention that allowed women to enter offices?
    (a) Typewriter
    (b) Knitting machine
    (c) Computer
    (d) Telephone

36. Who created the first free e-mail service 'Hotmail'?
    (a) Sabeer Bhatia
    (b) N. R. Narayana Murthy
    (c) William Gates
    (d) Steve Jobs

37. Which is the first mammal to be cloned in the world?
    (a) Sheep   (b) Pig
    (c) Mule   (d) Buffalo

38. Who led the first Indian expedition to Antarctica?
    (a) G.S. Sirohi   (b) S. Z. Qasim
    (c) P. S. Sehra   (d) V. K. Raina

II

INVENTORS

Inventions : Electrical, Mechanical

39. Who is the inventor of the printing press?
    - (a) Gail Borden
    - (b) R. W. Thomson
    - (c) Johann Guttenburg
    - (d) R. R. Bennett

40. Who is the inventor of the jet aircraft?
    - (a) Frank Whittle
    - (b) Wright brothers
    - (c) Otto Lillienthal
    - (d) Vannevar Bush

41. Who invented the telephone?
    - (a) Alexander G. Bell
    - (b) J. L. Baird
    - (c) Nicola Tesla
    - (d) James Dewar

42. Who invented the radio valve?
    - (a) William Shockley
    - (b) John Brattain
    - (c) Lee De Forest
    - (d) Jack Kilby

43. Who invented the turbine?
    (a) Charles Parson   (b) Rudolf Diesel
    (c) George Westinghouse (d) Robert Fulton

44. Who invented the thermos flask?
    (a) Eugene Goldstein   (b) Oliver Lodge
    (c) Denis Papin   (d) James Dewar

45. Who invented the airship?
    (a) Montgolfier brothers
    (b) Ferdinand Zeppelin
    (c) Auguste Piccard   (d) Jules Verne

46. Who invented the sewing machine?
    (a) Elias Howe   (b) William Thomas
    (c) I. M. Singer   (d) Heinrich Geissler

47. Who invented the railway engine?
    (a) Richard Trevithick (b) George Stephenson
    (c) Eli Whitney   (d) W. H. F. Talbot

48. Who invented the safety pin?
    (a) Charles Goodyear   (b) Stewart Harshone
    (c) Walter Hunt   (d) A. Rose

49. Who invented the telescope?
    (a) Galileo Galilei   (b) Hans Lippershey
    (c) Robert Hooke   (d) Hipparchus

50. Who invented the slide rule?
    - (a) Blaise Pascal
    - (b) William Oughtred
    - (c) Pierre Laplace
    - (d) John Napier

51. Who invented carbon dioxide laser?
    - (a) Charles Townes
    - (b) C. K. N. Patel
    - (c) Vikram Sarabhai
    - (d) Robert Noyce

52. Who invented the logarithm?
    - (a) George Boole
    - (b) John Napier
    - (c) Blaise Pascal
    - (d) Carl Gauss

53. Who invented the 'superbug' to remove oil pollution from the seas?
    - (a) P. M. Bhargava
    - (b) A. M. Chakrabarty
    - (c) Stephen Jay Gould
    - (d) Robert Gallo

54. Who invented zero?
    - (a) Varahamihira
    - (b) Aristotle
    - (c) Bhaskara
    - (d) None

55. Who invented some devices for underwater photography and filming?
    - (a) David Attenborough
    - (b) Jacques-Yves Cousteau
    - (c) Arthur C. Clarke
    - (d) Jacques Monod

56. Who invented the radar?
    (a) Karl Jansky
    (b) Robert Watson – Watt
    (c) Thomas Edison   (d) G. Marconi

57. Who invented the computer mouse?
    (a) Charles Babbage   (b) Douglas Engelbert
    (c) Steve Wozniak   (d) Vincent Cerf

Inventions: Chemicals

58. Who is the inventor of photography?
    (a) Louis Daguerre   (b) John Herschel
    (c) Mathew Brady   (d) Nikolaus Otto

59. Who invented the method of manufacturing steel from iron?
    (a) Henry Bessmer   (b) Robert Fulton
    (c) Thomas Andrews   (d) Samuel Crompton

60. Who invented the celluloid film which made movies possible?
    (a) Sidney W. Fox   (b) George Eastman
    (c) William Friese-Greene
    (d) Samuel Langley

61. Who invented cement used in buildings?
    (a) Joseph Aspdin
    (b) Charles Boyle
    (c) Elisha Otis
    (d) W. H. F. Talbot

62. Who invented the electric battery?
    (a) Alexendro Volta
    (b) Andre Ampere
    (c) Benjamin Franklin
    (d) Luigi Galvani

63. Who is the inventor of synthetic dyes?
    (a) Ernest Solvay
    (b) William Perkins
    (c) Karl Graebe
    (d) Fritz Haber

64. Who invented 'Bakelite' – the first commercially
    successful thermosetting plastic resin?
    (a) L. H. Backeland
    (b) Johann Baeyer
    (c) Melvin Calvin
    (d) John Larson

65. Who is the inventor of dynamite and blasting gela-
    tin?
    (a) Henry Cavendish
    (b) Antoine Lavoisier
    (c) Alfred Nobel
    (d) Humphry Davy

66. Who invented artificial silk?
    (a) Joseph W. Swan
    (b) John Wells
    (c) Roslyn D. Young
    (d) Frank F. Jewett

III

INSTRUMENTS, DEVICES AND EXPERIMENTS

Instruments

67. Where is the most powerful electron microscope installed ?
    (a) USA
    (b) West Germany
    (c) Japan
    (d) UK

68. Which one is used in determining the structure of molecules?
    (a) Mass spectroscopy (b) X-ray crystallography
    (c) Nuclear magnetic resonance
    (d) All

69. Which instrument is used for measuring the temperature variation at a place during the day?
    (a) Six's Maximum and Minimum thermometer
    (b) Clinical thermometer
    (c) Altimeter
    (d) Bolometer

70. Where is the most powerful accelerator – the atom-smasher installed ?
    (a) Geneva, Switzerland (b) Illinois, USA
    (c) Berkeley, USA   (d) Bonn, Germany

71. Which is used for navigating a ship?
    (a) Aneroid barometer (b) Sonometer
    (c) Telescope   (d) Sextant

72. Which instrument is used for determining the elements present in a substance?
    (a) Microscope   (b) Periscope
    (c) Spectroscope   (d) Magnetometer

73. Which instrument is used for measuring the heart-beat of a person?
    (a) Voltmeter   (b) Cardiogram
    (c) Stethoscope   (d) Altimeter

74. Where is the world's largest radio telescope located?
    (a) Cambridge, UK   (b) Puerto Rico, USA
    (c) New Mexico   (d) Westerbork, Netherlands

75. Which instrument is used for measuring the atmospheric pressure at a place?
    (a) Barometer   (b) Hygrometer
    (c) Anemometer   (d) Thermometer

76. Which instrument is used to determine the density of a liquid?
    - (a) Hydrometer
    - (b) Hygrometer
    - (c) Galvanometer
    - (d) Sonometer

77. Which instrument is used for checking up whether a cell is generating current or not?
    - (a) Microscope
    - (b) Magnetic compass
    - (c) Galvanometer
    - (d) Spectroscope

78. Which instrument determines how much a vehicle has travelled?
    - (a) Speedometer
    - (b) Barometer
    - (c) Ammeter
    - (d) Milometer

79. Which instrument is used for recording earthquakes?
    - (a) Telegraph
    - (b) Micrometer
    - (c) Seismograph
    - (d) Spectrograph

80. Where is the world's largest optical telescope located?
    - (a) Mount Palomar, USA
    - (b) Mount Semirodriki, USSR
    - (c) Mount Hopkins, USA
    - (d) Mauna Kea, Hawaii

Devices

81. What does an electric bell work on?
    (a) Electromagnetic induction
    (b) Electrochemical reactions
    (c) Magnetism
    (d) Electric charges

82. If there is too much light in the surrounding and one wants to take a photograph, what will one use?
    (a) Filter
    (b) Flash
    (c) Screen
    (d) Reflector

83. What should not be kept near a tape recorder?
    (a) Clock
    (b) Magnet
    (c) Electrical switchboard
    (d) Radio

84. What does a Xerox machine work on?
    (a) Electromagnetic image-making
    (b) Electrostatic image-making
    (c) Magnetic image-making
    (d) Thermal image-making

85. What should be kept handy in case there is a short circuit?
    (a) Fuse wire
    (b) Galvanometer
    (c) Transistor
    (d) Ammeter

86. If a computer is kept at home, what should be checked?
    (a) Electricity leakage   (b) Voltage fluctuations
    (c) Traffic in the area   (d) Water leakage

87. If this crucial component is not working, a vehicle
    will not move. What is it?
    (a) Milometer   (b) Horn
    (c) Spark plug   (d) Brake

88. During a nuclear war what kind of energy would
    destroy all electronic devices whether in hospital,
    aircrafts or homes?
    (a) Nuclear radiation   (b) Heat
    (c) Ultraviolet rays   (d) Electronic pulse

89. What is a filament made of in an ordinary light bulb?
    (a) Tungsten   (b) Platinum
    (c) Lead   (d) Carbon

90. Which substance in a fluorescent tube converts an
    electric glow into luminous light?
    (a) Phosphor   (b) Mercury chloride
    (c) Silica   (d) Lime

91. What does an electric cell work on?
    (a) Electrochemical reactions
    (b) Solar energy
    (c) Electromagnetic induction
    (d) Magnetism

Experiments

92. Which experiment not only measured the velocity of light accurately but also dealt a death blow to the ether theory once and for all?
    (a) Michelson–Morley experiment
    (b) Fizeau experiment
    (c) Weber experiment
    (d) Einstein experiment

93. Who conducted the most imaginary 'Elevator' experiment which led to a revolutionary theory?
    (a) Nicolaus Copernicus (b) Wolfgang Pauli
    (c) George F. Fitzgerald (d) Albert Einstein

94. Louis Pasteur conducted a famous experiment to prove the germ theory of diseases. What was the crucial apparatus in the experiment?
    (a) Liebig condenser   (b) Heater
    (c) Flask with an S-shaped neck
    (d) Jar with a round bottom

95. Which living organism Barbara McClintock used for her experiments that led to the discovery of 'Jumping genes'?
    (a) Rabbits   (b) Fruit flies
    (c) Corn   (d) Peas

96. Who conducted the first experiment that proved that life on earth could be the result of chemical evolution?
    (a) Stanley L. Miller   (b) H. C. Urey
    (c) J.B.S. Haldane   (d) Robert Koch

97. Frank Drake was the first to make an attempt to direct radio signals at a star, announcing our presence on earth. Which was that star?
    (a) Tau Ceti   (b) Bernard's star
    (c) Alpha Centauri   (d) Proxima Centauri

98. Who conducted the experiment that produced vacuum for the first time?
    (a) E. Torricelli   (b) Blaise Pascal
    (c) Charles Boyle   (d) Lord Rayleigh

99. Eratosthenes measured the size of the earth by measuring shadows of bodies in the sun in two cities. Which were the two cities?
    (a) Alexandria and Baghdad
    (b) Alexandria and Syene
    (c) Alexandria and Syracuse
    (d) Syene and Syracuse

100. Benjamin Franklin discovered electricity in lightning. What did he use to discover it?
    (a) Kite   (b) Electrostat
    (c) Galvanometer   (d) Lightning conductor

101. Where was conducted the famous experiment that showed both heavy and light bodies take the same time to fall down to the earth?
    (a) Empire State Building
    (b) Eiffel Tower
    (c) Leaning Tower of Pisa
    (d) Qutab Minar

102. What proved Albert Einstein's general theory of relativity to be experimentally correct?
    (a) Space shuttle   (b) Cyclotron
    (c) Solar eclipse   (d) Lunar eclipse

IV

METALS AND MINERALS

Metals

103. Which is the most abundant metal in the earth's crust?
    (a) Iron
    (b) Lead
    (c) Copper
    (d) Aluminium

104. Plants are not able to fix nitrogen from air to produce proteins when a metal is not present in very minute quantities. Which metal is it?
    (a) Copper
    (b) Gallium
    (c) Zirconium
    (d) Molydbenum

105. Where lies the biggest deposit of gold?
    (a) Kolar, India
    (b) Muruntau, Russia
    (c) Ballarat, Australia
    (d) Witwatersrand. South Africa

106. Which metals make bronze alloy?
   (a) Aluminium, copper and tin
   (b) Copper, tin and cobalt
   (c) Zinc, tin and copper
   (d) Tin, aluminium and nickel

107. Even the so-called pure gold contains a metal in small amount. Which metal is it?
   (a) Sodium   (b) Copper
   (c) Tin ·   (d) Magnesium

108. Which is the most widely used metal?
   (a) Copper   (b) Aluminium
   (c) Iron   (d) Gold

109. Which element imparts corrosion-resistance to steel?
   (a) Nitrogen   (b) Nickel
   (c) Tungsten   (d) Magnesium

110. Which is the metal as strong as steel but half as much in weight?
   (a) Mercury   (b) Titanium
   (c) Aluminium   (d) Platinum

111. Where was the technique of powder metallurgy invented?
   (a) Germany   (b) United Kingdom
   (c) Greece   (d) India

112. Which natural source will be tapped for the large scale extraction of valuable metals in the near future?
    (a) Red sea muds   (b) Coral reefs
    (c) Polymetallic nodules
    (d) Volcanoes

113. Which is the metal that remains liquid at room temperature?
    (a) Platinum   (b) Chromium
    (c) Tungsten   (d) Mercury

114. Which metal's container is least affected by acids present in foods?
    (a) Iron   (b) Aluminium
    (c) Copper   (d) Zinc

115. Which is the first alloy, a mixture of two metals, to be made in the world?
    (a) Duralumin   (b) Brass
    (c) Stainless steel   (d) Bronze

Minerals

116. Which mineral is nicknamed 'fool's gold ' because its yellow colour often confuses gold prospectors?
    (a) Pyrite   (b) Galena
    (c) Fluorite   (d) Silica

117. Which mineral gets deposited as 'furs' in boiling pots, kettles, etc. in region where hard-water is available?
    (a) Pyroxene   (b) Halite
    (c) Mica   (d) Calcite

118. Which type of rocks is used for making roofs of houses?
    (a) Gniess   (b) Slate
    (c) Basalt   (d) Granite

119. Which mineral is often used as an abrasive?
    (a) Fluorite   (b) Mica
    (c) Feldspar   (d) Corundum

120. Which mineral is used in jewellery?
    (a) Mica   (b) Garnet
    (c) Halite   (d) None

121. Which mineral is used in making plaster and paper?
    (a) Gypsum   (b) Feldspar
    (c) Silica   (d) None

122. Which rock is used as stones for building houses?
    (a) Oolite   (b) Shale
    (c) Breccia   (d) Hornfels

123. Where do natural diamonds occur?
    (a) Fluorite   (b) Covellite
    (c) Diallage   (d) Kimberlite

124. Which mineral was used for making compass in the past?
    (a) Gypsum   (b) Haematite
    (c) Magnetite   (d) Feldspar

125. Which mineral ore forms kidney-shaped crystals?
    (a) Pyrite   (b) Silica
    (c) Haematite   (d) Galena

V

NATURAL PHENOMENA

Nature's Doings

126. Which phenomenon occurring on the surface of the sun is an optical illusion?
    (a) Solar flares   (b) Sunspots
    (c) Spicules   (d) None

127. What has natural, exquisite crystal-like structure?
    (a) Meteorites   (b) Snow-flakes
    (c) Rain drops   (d) None

128. Where are observed the quiet, windless zones called 'doldrums' on the surface of the earth?
    (a) South Pole
    (b) Between 60 degree South and 30 degree South
    (c) North Pole   (d) About the equator

129. Which natural phenomenon is known in Sanskrit as 'deer's thirst'?
- (a) Rainbow
- (b) Earthshine
- (c) Halo
- (d) Mirage

130. What is basically a shooting star?
- (a) Meteor
- (b) Supernova
- (c) Comet tail
- (d) Disturbance in atmosphere

131. Which natural phenomenon is based on the refraction of light?
- (a) Rainbow
- (b) Polar light
- (c) Earth light
- (d) Lightning

132. Where does one hear the lowest noise?
- (a) Tropical forest
- (b) Broadcasting studio
- (c) Desert
- (d) Living room

133. Which phenomenon occurs when certain disturbances take place in the sun?
- (a) Mirages
- (b) Hailstorms
- (c) Magnetic storms
- (d) Dust storms

134. When is a green flash seen?
- (a) During lightning
- (b) During a solar flare
- (c) During sunrise and sunset
- (d) During a volcanic eruption

135. What falls continuously down on the entire surface of the earth, whether it is day or night?
    (a) Rain
    (b) Meteors
    (c) Cosmic rays
    (d) Solar wind

136. What is the origin of zodiacal light?
    (a) Volcanoes
    (b) Ice crystals in the air
    (c) Dust cloud beyond the earth
    (d) Cosmic rays

Meteorology

137. Where does the 'Indian summer' occur?
    (a) Russia
    (b) India
    (c) UK
    (d) Borneo

138. Which meteorology phenomenon can cause damage to crops?
    (a) Hail
    (b) Rains
    (c) Dew
    (d) Duststorm

139. Which phenomenon occurs mostly in the USA and its neighbouring countries?
    (a) Cyclone
    (b) Duststorm
    (c) Magnetic storm
    (d) Tornado

140. What is the origin of word 'Monsoon'?
    (a) Arabic 'Season'   (b) Greek 'Weather'
    (c) Latin 'Clouds'   (d) None

141. Which meteorological phenomenon occurs frequently over the Bay of Bengal?
    (a) Tornado   (b) Cyclone
    (c) El Nino   (d) None

142. What is found on grass and flowers early in the morning?
    (a) Mist   (b) Ice
    (c) Dew   (d) Dust

143. Thunderstorms and lightnings deliver a large amount of a particular element to the air and soil. What is that?
    (a) Sodium   (b) Nitrogen
    (c) Sulphur   (d) Oxygen

144. Which phenomenon can affect weather conditions on the earth?
    (a) Earthquakes   (b) Volcanoes
    (c) Falling meteorites   (d) None

145. What kind of phenomenon is ball lightning?
    (a) Heat   (b) Magnetic
    (c) Electric   (d) All

146. Where does the most dangerous hot wind 'Fohn', which burns villages and melts snow occur?
    (a) Sahara
    (b) Siberia
    (c) Switzerland
    (d) Iran

147. To what extent does temperature fall as one goes up above the surface of the earth?
    (a) – 10 degree Celsius (b) – 23 degree Celsius
    (c) – 108 degree Celsius
    (d) – 62 degree Celsius

148. Which layer of atmosphere protects life on the earth from harmful radiations coming from the sun and space?
    (a) Ozone layer
    (b) Ionosphere
    (c) Mesosphere
    (d) Troposphere

149. Monsoon on the Indian subcontinent is controlled by some phenomenon occurring over a region. Which region is it?
    (a) African continent
    (b) Indian Ocean
    (c) Antarctica
    (d) North Pole

VI

EVOLUTION AND BEHAVIOUR

Evolution

150. What is the strong evidence that all living things have a common origin?
    (a) Found on the same planet.
    (b) The homology concept.
    (c) One theory of the evolution of life.
    (d) No life detected outside the earth.

151. Which is called a 'living fossil' – a fish once found in abundance in ancient seas?
    (a) Herring   (b) Shark
    (c) Coelacanth   (d) Snapper

152. When did birds evolve?
    (a) Jurassic period   (b) Permian period
    (c) Silurian period   (d) Quaternary period

153. Where are the oldest fossils found?
   (a) North Pole, Northwest Australia
   (b) Alice Springs, Central Australia
   (c) Ediacaran hills, Southern Australia
   (d) Mazon Creek, Illinois, USA

154. Which living being is the most abundant on the earth today?
   (a) Bird   (b) Beetle
   (c) Reptile   (d) Fish

155. When did mammals evolve?
   (a) Cambrian period   (b) Tertiary period
   (c) Triassic period   (d) Jurassic period

156. Which tree is called a 'living fossil' – a tree once found in abundance in ancient times?
   (a) Maidenhair   (b) Fig
   (c) Mimosa   (d) Osier

157. Which of the following is often associated with the theory of evolution of life propounded by Charles Darwin?
   (a) H.M.S. Beagle
   (b) Essay on the principle of population
   (c) Galapagos islands   (d) All

158. When did the maximum amount of extinction of life take place?
    (a) Cretaceous
    (b) Carboniferous
    (c) Pleistocene
    (d) Cambrian

159. Who propounded that life could have originated from a chemical soup?
    (a) A. I. Oparin
    (b) J. B. S. Haldane
    (c) Both
    (d) None

160. Which creature's fossils are the oldest yet discovered?
    (a) Cyanobacteria
    (b) Pelagic graptolites
    (c) Stromatolites
    (d) Trilobites

161. Who propounded the theory of evolution at the same time as Charles Darwin did?
    (a) Asa Grey
    (b) Thomas Malthus
    (c) T. H. Huxley
    (d) Alfred R. Wallace

162. Which is not a living fossil?
    (a) Pearly nautilus
    (b) Velvet worm
    (c) Horseshoe crab
    (d) Dragonfly

Behaviour

163. What is studying the behaviour of animals in the wild called?
    (a) Eugenics
    (b) Ethology
    (c) Behavioural psychology
    (d) Sociobiology

164. Which creature can locate its prey in the dark by sensing infra-red 'heat' rays?
   (a) Bats
   (b) Owl
   (c) Fox
   (d) Rattlesnake

165. In recent years, the population of the herring gull has increased considerably and so also its geographical distribution. Why?
   (a) Conservation efforts.
   (b) Food available in rubbish dumps.
   (c) Abundance of food in oceans.
   (d) Genetics.

166. Which animal rarely mates with its close relatives despite living together?
   (a) Wild dogs
   (b) Prairie dogs
   (c) Zebras
   (d) Deer

167. A Thomson's gazelle flees from wild dogs when they come within 500 to 1000 metres of it. It however flees from a cheetah only when it comes as close as 100 to 300 metres. Why?
   (a) A cheetah is not as ferocious as wild dogs.
   (b) A cheetah can run very fast in short spurts only.
   (c) A cheetah runs faster than wild dogs.
   (d) Unlike wild dogs a cheetah attack alone.

168. Which animal does 'baby-sitting' for its fellows?
    (a) Gazelle   (b) Deer
    (c) Gray meerkat   (d) Baboon

169. 'You pat my back, and I pat yours'. What is it called in the animal world?
    (a) Parasitism   (b) Commensalism
    (c) Symbiosis   (d) None of these

170. Which animal builds a nest?
    (a) Wildebeest   (b) Wild boar
    (c) Elephant   (d) None

171. Why have rats survived all attempts to eradicate them?
    (a) Rats are quick to avoid a bait once found to have unpleasant effects.
    (b) No poison exists to kill all rats.
    (c) Rats can recognise a bait.
    (d) Rats can communicate information about a poisoned bait to each other.

VII

FISH AND INSECTS

Fish

172. How long can a sperm whale hold its breath during a dive?
    (a) 5 hours
    (b) 2 hours
    (c) 35 minutes
    (d) 15 minutes

173. Which fish is used to catch turtles?
    (a) Sucker fish
    (b) Giant gourami
    (c) Angler fish
    (d) Barracuda

174. Which fish is found in the rivers of Indo-Gangetic plains?
    (a) Indian tarpon
    (b) Indian trout
    (c) Pomfret
    (d) Minnow

175. Which fish was introduced in India to act as a biological control for the eradication of malaria?
    (a) Gambusia
    (b) Milk fish
    (c) Mackerel
    (d) Mahseer

176. Which is the most expensive and highly edible fish in the Indian market?
    (a) Catla
    (b) Rohu
    (c) Milkfish
    (d) Pomfret

177. Which fish hangs a bait for its prey?
    (a) Barracuda
    (b) Angler fish
    (c) Rohu
    (d) Hilsa

178. Which is the largest invertebrate in the world?
    (a) Giant squid
    (b) Octopus
    (c) Giant clam
    (d) Star fish

179. Which is an air-breathing fish?
    (a) Mud-skipper
    (b) Cat fish
    (c) Eel
    (d) Salmon

180. Which type of fish covers the sea for miles together and is a wonderful sight to see?
    (a) Dwarf gourami
    (b) Carp
    (c) Jelly fish
    (d) Catfish

181. Which fish is a hazard to swimmers?
    (a) Catla
    (b) Giant gourami
    (c) Portuguese man-of-war
    (d) Blind fish

182. Which is the largest fish?
    (a) Whale shark
    (b) Mackeral
    (c) Swordfish
    (d) Baleen whale

183. Which is the fastest swimmer?
    (a) Sailfish
    (b) Salmon
    (c) Octopus
    (d) Seal

184. Which fish is often grown in tanks and acclaimed as an excellent food?
    (a) Carp
    (b) Minnow
    (c) Mahseer
    (d) Milkfish

Insects

185. What is the shape of a honeybee's cell?
    (a) Circular
    (b) Square
    (c) Triangular
    (d) Hexagon

186. Which insect grows its own food?
    (a) Honeybee
    (b) Bumblebee
    (c) Leaf cutter ant
    (d) Dung beetle

187. Which insect is seen dancing in a swarm over or near water?
    (a) Caddis fly
    (b) Mayfly
    (c) Water spider
    (d) Ant

188. What are known as 'book scorpions'?
    (a) Silverfish   (b) False spider
    (c) Caterpillar   (d) Scorpion spider

189. Which insect is often seen near ponds or streams?
    (a) Cockroach   (b) Butterfly
    (c) Wasp   (d) Caddis fly

190. Which habitat is most favourable to butterflies?
    (a) Desert   (b) Tundra
    (c) Tropical forest   (d) Savanna

191. Which is the group of butterflies that are the largest
    and the most beautiful?
    (a) Skippers   (b) Browns
    (c) Swallowtails   (d) Whites

192. Which insect is mostly a night-flier?
    (a) Butterfly   (b) Moth
    (c) Honeybee   (d) Lacewings

193. Which insect has more species than all the other
    animal life put together?
    (a) Beetle   (b) Antlion
    (c) Thrip   (d) Mosquito

194. Honeybee performs dance of a particular shape to communicate to others the source of nectar. What is that shape?
    (a) Figure of 6   (b) Pentagon
    (c) Figure of 8   (d) Hexagon

195. Which insect has the largest population on earth?
    (a) Flea   (b) Wasp
    (c) Bug   (d) Fly

196. Which insect loves books?
    (a) Silverfish   (b) Bug
    (c) Caddis fly   (d) Beetle

197. Which insect is harmful to man both healthwise and economywise?
    (a) Flea   (b) Louse
    (c) Mosquito   (d) Cockroach

198. Which is the largest butterfly?
    (a) Red Admiral butterfly
    (b) Monarch butterfly
    (c) Queen Alexandra birdwing
    (d) Passion vine butterfly

41

VIII

INDIAN WILDLIFE, BIRDS AND LANDSCAPE

Wildlife

199. Where is Project Tiger in progress?
    (a) Jaldapara
    (b) Bharatpur
    (c) Melghat
    (d) Dachigam

200. Dachigam sanctuary is the last refuge of an animal. Which one?
    (a) Cheetah
    (b) Hangul
    (c) Giraffe
    (d) Lion

201. Which animal is dreaded as a 'baby-lifter'?
    (a) Panther
    (b) Lynx
    (c) Lion-tailed macaque
    (d) Hyena

202. Where is rhino found?
   (a) West Bengal
   (b) Kerala
   (c) Chattisgarh
   (d) Bihar

203. Which animal hunts its prey in a pack?
   (a) Red fox
   (b) Dhole
   (c) Hanuman langur
   (d) Pika

204. Where is marbled cat found?
   (a) Himachal Pradesh
   (b) Uttaranchal
   (c) Assam
   (d) Karnatka

205. Which of the following animals found in India is an endangered species?
   (a) Asiatic wild ass
   (b) Langur
   (c) Hyena
   (d) Tiger

206. Which is the most common primate in India?
   (a) Hanuman Langur
   (b) Purple faced Langur
   (c) Nilgiri Langur
   (d) Golden Langur

207. Which animal found in India has become almost extinct?
   (a) Black buck
   (b) Gaur
   (c) Cheetah
   (d) Chevrotain

208. Where is Red Panda found?
    (a) Nilgiris   (b) Himalayas
    (c) Sundarbans   (d) Vindhyas

209. Which wild goat seen in India often lives at great
     altitudes near the snowline?
    (a) Tahr   (b) Ibex
    (c) Goral   (d) Serow

210. Where is snow leopard found?
    (a) Western ghats   (b) Mount Abu
    (c) Himalayas   (d) Deccan traps

211. Which national park is the first to be established in
     India in 1935?
    (a) Corbett National Park
    (b) Keoladeo National Park
    (c) Kaziranga National Park
    (d) Dudhwa National Park

212. Where is the crocodile bank in the country located?
    (a) Srinagar   (b) Sundarbans
    (c) Chennai   (d) Balasore

213. Which deer found in India has no antlers and has
     tusk-like incisors?
    (a) Musk deer   (b) Barking deer
    (c) Swamp deer   (d) Hog deer

44

214. Where is the Point Calimere sanctuary located ?
    (a) Kihim bay   (b) Coromandel coast
    (c) Gulf of Kutch   (d) Himalayan foothills

215. Gir forest in Gujarat is the last home of an animal.
    Which one?
    (a) Tiger   (b) Cheetah
    (c) Indian Lion   (d) Indian Leopard

Birds

216. Which stork is also a scavenger?
    (a) Painted stork   (b) Open-billed stork
    (c) Adjutant stork   (d) White stork

217. Which bird likes performing dust-baths frequently
    to keep its feathers in good condition?
    (a) Sparrow   (b) Kestrel
    (c) Black Ibis   (d) Darter

218. Which bird has a melodious, flutelike call?
    (a) Coppersmith   (b) Oriole
    (c) Dabchick   (d) Indian pipit

219. Which bird is nocturnal in habit?
    (a) Nightjar   (b) Sarus crane
    (c) Brahminy myna   (d) House swift

220. Which bird has spidery toes and long hind-claws?
    (a) Red-vented bulbul   (b) Water cock
    (c) White wagtail   (d) Pheasant tailed jacana

221. Which bird has a musical whistling call?
    (a) Stone curlew   (b) Common starling
    (c) Iora   (d) Little green bee-eater

222. Which of the following water birds prefer salt lakes?
    (a) Moorhen   (b) Coot
    (c) Sarus crane   (d) Flamingo

223. Which of the following ducks has become extinct?
    (a) Pink-headed duck   (b) Whistling duck
    (c) Cotton teal   (d) Nakta

224. Which bird is often seen in a party of seven?
    (a) Indian tit   (b) Babbler
    (c) Shrike   (d) Crow

225. Which bird's call sounds like 'Did-you-do-it'?
    (a) Little ringed plover   (b) Green barbet
    (c) Red-whiskered bulbul
    (d) Red-wattled lapwing

Landscape

226. Which lake in India was once a part of the sea?
    (a) Dal lake   (b) Chilka lake
    (c) Sultanpur lake   (d) Vihar lake

227. Which region of the continental shelf around India contains oils and natural gas?
    (a) Off Cochin   (b) Off Kolkata
    (c) Off Puri   (d) Off Mumbai

228. Which Indian state has the largest number of doabs – alluvial tracts of land between two rivers?
    (a) Punjab   (b) Karnataka
    (c) Chattisgarh   (d) Assam

229. Which geological formation in India is a result of volcanic eruptions?
    (a) Deccan traps   (b) Himalayas
    (c) Vindhya mountains   (d) Satpura range

230. Which are the oldest mountains in India?
    (a) Vindhyas   (b) Himalayas
    (c) Aravallis   (d) Sahyadris

231. Which are the folded mountains in India?
    (a) Nilgiris   (b) Sahyadris
    (c) Himalayas   (d) None

232. Which state of India is largely an alluvial plain?
    (a) Meghalaya
    (b) Himachal Pradesh
    (c) Manipur
    (d) Punjab

233. Which is the large brackish-water lagoon near an Indian city?
    (a) Pulicat lake
    (b) Chilka lake
    (c) Sambar lake
    (d) Silsit lake

234. Where are natural caves found in India?
    (a) Tripura
    (b) Uttar Pradesh
    (c) Nagaland
    (d) Haryana

235. Where are 'bhabar' lands in India located?
    (a) Near Sivalik hills
    (b) Deccan traps
    (c) Near Western ghats
    (d) Andhra Pradesh

236. Which is the highest mountain entirely within Indian territory?
    (a) Mount Everest
    (b) Nanda Devi
    (c) Kanchenjunga
    (d) Karakoram

237. Which lake in India is essentially a crater?
    (a) Dal lake
    (b) Bhim Tal
    (c) Sambar lake
    (d) Lonar lake

IX

ESSENTIAL SCIENCES

Mathematics

238. Which is the Ramanujan number?
    (a) 1163   (b) 1723
    (c) 2234   (d) 1952

239. Which is Kaprekar's number?
    (a) 6785   (b) 2435
    (c) 6174   (d) All

240. What was the original term for zero?
    (a) Zephr   (b) Sunya
    (c) Sifr   (d) Cipher

241. What is the source of our knowledge of Egyptian mathematics?
    (a) Rhind Papyrus   (b) Pharoah's tombs
    (c) Both   (d) None

242. Zero plays a vital role in the working of one device. Which one?
   (a) Abacus   (b) Computer
   (c) Transistor   (d) Clock

243. Where was the concept of negative numbers invented?
   (a) Arab   (b) India
   (c) Italy   (d) Greece

244. Which geometrical object has one surface and one edge?
   (a) Cube   (b) Mobius strip
   (c) Cone   (d) Cylinder

245. Gambling is also a subject of study of one branch of mathematics. Which one?
   (a) Probability   (b) Topology
   (c) Mensuration   (d) Trigonometry

246. Which subject is often the butt of everyone's jokes because it can be manipulated to show the desired results?
   (a) Projective geometry
   (b) Calculus
   (c) Statistics   (d) Algebra

247. What are these numbers – 1, 1, 2, 3, 5, 8, 13, 21,
    .... — known as?
    (a) Fictitious numbers   (b) Fibonacci numbers
    (c) Fermat numbers   (d) Prime numbers

248. What is this known as?

$$1$$
$$1 \quad 1$$
$$1 \quad 2 \quad 1$$
$$1 \quad 3 \quad 3 \quad 1$$
$$1 \quad 4 \quad 6 \quad 4 \quad 1$$

    (a) Abracadabdra   (b) Magic triangle
    (c) Pascal's triangle   (d) Gauss's triangle

249. Which branch of mathematics has truth table?
    (a) Computer logic   (b) Geometry
    (c) Spherical trigonometry
    (d) Algebra

Geography

250. Where is the hottest spring in the world located?
    (a) Yellowstone National Park, USA
    (b) Kulu, Himachal Pradesh, India
    (c) Tooral, Maharashtra, India
    (d) Lasundra, Gujarat, India

251. Which is the world's most remote, and inhabited island?
    (a) Tristan da Cunha   (b) Seychelles
    (c) Nicobar   (d) Maldives

252. Which is the largest brackish water region?
    (a) Baltic sea   (b) Red sea
    (c) Lake Baikal   (d) Caspian sea

253. Where has the world's largest cave been discovered?
    (a) China   (b) Southeast Asia
    (c) India   (d) Spain

254. Which city is nearest to the Great Barrier Reef – the biggest reef in the world?
    (a) Canberra   (b) California
    (c) Brisbane   (d) Honolulu

255. What is the band of ocean between 50 degrees South and 69 degrees South known as?
    (a) The Roaring Forties
    (b) The Antarctic Conver gence
    (c) The Equator   (d) Horse Latitude

256. Where has the oldest rock on earth been found?
    (a) Damodar river valley, India
    (b) Lake Baikal, Russia.
    (c) Minnesota river valley, USA
    (d) Gabon, South Africa

257. Which is the deepest freshwater lake in the world?
    (a) Lake Titikaka   (b) Lake Sambar
    (c) Lake Baikal   (d) Lake Chilka

258. Which is the continent covered with ice?
    (a) Arctic   (b) Antarctica
    (c) Greenland   (d) Iceland

Agriculture

259. Which food crop has the maximum content of proteins?
    (a) Cassava   (b) Soyabean
    (c) Wheat   (d) Maize

260. How much per cent of the earth's surface could be used for growing food?
    (a) One per cent   (b) Fifty three per cent
    (c) Eighty two per cent (d) Eleven per cent

261. Which four crops are produced in an amount more than the combined production of other food crops?
    (a) Wheat, oat, potato and soyabean
    (b) Barley, oat, rice and rye
    (c) Wheat, maize, potato and rice
    (d) Rice, potato, rye and maize

262. Since time immemorial, India is renowned for her cultivation of a plant. Which is it?
    (a) Cotton   (b) Wheat
    (c) Tea   (d) Cocoa

263. Which element is depleted most from the soil after a crop is harvested?
    (a) Calcium   (b) Potassium
    (c) Phosphorus   (d) Zinc

264. Cocoa tree is the source of natural chocolate flavour. Which part of the tree is the source?
    (a) Seeds   (b) Leaves
    (c) Stem   (d) Flower

265. Which food item basically originated in India?
    (a) Clover   (b) Cardamom
    (c) Potato   (d) Date

266. Which vegetable is the fruiting body of a fungus?
    (a) Cauliflower   (b) Radish
    (c) Mushroom   (d) Spinach

267. Which chemical used in agriculture contains nitrogen, potassium and phosphorus?
    (a) Herbicide   (b) Fertilizer
    (c) Pesticide   (d) None

268. Of the twenty different species of wheat, how many are commercially being grown for the production of food?
   (a) Five   (b) One
   (c) Two   (d) All

269. Where did potato, one of the major human foods, originate?
   (a) India   (b) Chile
   (c) Ireland   (d) Germany

270. Which vegetable is grown throughout the world?
   (a) Cucumber   (b) Carrot
   (c) Jackfruit   (d) None

271. Which element is used as a fungicide?
   (a) Sulphur   (b) Potassium
   (c) Carbon   (d) Calcium

272. Which of the following living beings is the most beneficial to farmers?
   (a) Earthworm   (b) Mouse
   (c) Weaver-bird   (d) None

273. Which type of agriculture is practised on mountains and hills?
   (a) Shifting cultivation   (b) Terrace cultivation
   (c) Intensive cultivation   (d) None

WOMAN OF ACHIEVEMENT -- Dr. Maria Goeppert Mayer, a professor of theoretical physics and chemistry teacher at the University of California in San Diego, has been called "the most distinguished woman scientist in the world." She is two discoveries concerning the structure and forces within the nucleus of the atom. In 1963 she shared a Nobel Prize in physics." She is the Nobel woman to win this honor in the field of science. (UPI-UPI). Accompanies X-NB-NAT.)

Q. 274 With mathematical calculations on the blackboard behind her and a slide-rule in her hand, who is this great nuclear physicist and Nobel Laureate?

Q. 275 A Bharat Ratna recipient, he had created a social revolution during his life-time. Who is this elderly Indian engineer?

Q. 276 He may be called the founder of the Silicon Valley in the US. Besides, he is the inventor of transistor and a Nobel Laureate. Who is he?

Q. 277 Surrounded with chemicals, this Indian-born Nobel Laureate is today a leading biochemist settled in the US. Who is he?

Q. 278 He is the inventor of vulcanised rubber, who spent his entire life in poverty. Who is he?

Q. 279 Who is this scholarly looking Indian scientist? He is the discoverer of microwaves and inventor of crescograph?

Q. 280 He laid the foundations of quantum physics. Who is he?

Q. 281 Who is this Indian statistician?

Q 282 Who is this smart-looking woman decorated with so many military medals and honours? She has achieved a first in the world.

Q. 283 An aerospace engineer, he is today the President of India. Who is he?

Q. 284 Who are these two well known radio astronomers? They discovered the proof of the presence of 'Big Bang' theory of origin of the universe.

Q. 285 A little known yet immortal scientist, a fundamental bio-chemical cycle is his discovery. Who is he?

XI

FRONTIER SCIENCES

Energy

286. Which nuclear fuel is now commonly used in nuclear reactors?
   - (a) Plutonium
   - (b) Uranium
   - (c) Thorium
   - (d) Lithium

287. Which country is the biggest consumer of energy?
   - (a) Russia
   - (b) France
   - (c) Canada
   - (d) USA

288. Which elementary particle acts like a 'trigger' for the generation of nuclear energy?
   - (a) Meson
   - (b) Proton
   - (c) Neutron
   - (d) Hepton

289. Which fuel runs a modern submarine?
   - (a) Nuclear fuel
   - (b) Petrol
   - (c) Coal
   - (d) Hydrogen

290. Which non-conventional energy source was once used on a large scale in the Netherlands?
    (a) Wind energy
    (b) Tidal energy
    (c) Wave energy
    (d) Ocean thermal energy

291. Which fuel is likely to be used on a large scale in the near future?
    (a) Wood
    (b) Petrol
    (c) Methane
    (d) Hydrogen

292. Which rays coming from the sun could be converted into electric energy for household needs?
    (a) Infrared rays
    (b) X-rays
    (c) Ultraviolet rays
    (d) Gamma rays

293. Which fuel creates the maximum amount of pollution, seen or unseen?
    (a) Nuclear fuel
    (b) Petrol
    (c) Coal
    (d) Wood

294. Which type of energy will solve the energy crisis of the world, provided certain 'critical conditions' necessary for it are sustained?
    (a) Fusion energy
    (b) Solar energy
    (c) Laser energy
    (d) Geothermal energy

295. What is heavy water, used in a nuclear reactor as a neutron moderator called?
   (a) Deuterium   (b) Protium
   (c) Tritium   (d) Helium

296. Which fuel is used to drive rockets?
   (a) Coal   (b) Uranium
   (c) Liquid hydrogen (d) Methanol

Computers

297. Which computer is often referred to as the granddaddy of computers?
   (a) ENIAC   (b) Analytical Engine
   (c) Pascaline   (d) Zuse III

298. Where is Silicon Valley located?
   (a) Higashi-Ku, Japan (b) Los Angeles, USA
   (c) Canterbury, UK   (d) Palo Alto, USA

299. Which computer language is the easiest to learn?
   (a) BASIC   (b) ADA
   (c) FORTRAN   (d) PL/1

300. When is a computer called 'user friendly'?
   (a) When it is presented to you by your friend.
   (b) When it is used by your friend.
   (c) When it needs a friend to use it.
   (d) When it functions like a friend.

301. What is a 'dedicated' computer?
    (a) It is dedicated to perform one type of task or tasks.
    (b) It is dedicated to its creator.
    (c) It is a very fast computer.
    (d) It performs its functions with dedication.

302. Which computer language is not a high-level language?
    (a) FORTRAN
    (b) COBOL
    (c) BASIC
    (d) None

303. What is known as the 'brain' of a computer?
    (a) Control Unit
    (b) Arithmetic Unit
    (c) Input Unit
    (d) Central Processing Unit

304. Which computer is called the first generation computer?
    (a) Cray
    (b) Apple
    (c) Leo
    (d) Plato

305. Which type of calculator is often referred to as the ancient computer?
    (a) Abacus
    (b) Napier's bones
    (c) Slide rule
    (d) Computer clock

306. Which is the latest material used for manufacturing a computer chip?
    (a) Silicon
    (b) Gallium Arsenide
    (c) Gallium Silicate
    (d) Carbon

307. What can a computer not do?
    (a) Abstract thought
    (b) Breaking coded messages
    (c) Analysing a situation
    (d) Writing poetry

Biotechnology

308. Which biochemical process has been used by man since time immemorial?
    (a) Fermentation
    (b) Tissue culture
    (c) Cloning
    (d) Genetic engineering

309. Which micro-organism has been genetically altered so that it can eat oil spills?
    (a) Escherichia coli
    (b) Pseudomonas
    (c) Entamoeba coli
    (d) Staphylococcus aureus

310. Biotechnology will produce a variety of fuels from a material. What is it?
    (a) Minerals
    (b) Air
    (c) Metals
    (d) Biomass

311. Which item will be genetically altered so that it can be used as a feed for animals and fishes?
    (a) Diatoms
    (b) Blue green algae
    (c) Molasses
    (d) Corn

312. Which type of pharmaceutical products will be most benefited by genetic engineering?
    (a) Antibiotics
    (b) Sulpha drugs
    (c) Antiseptics
    (d) Antidepressants

313. Biotechnology is likely to be used on a large scale for performing one of the following tasks. Which one?
    (a) Cleaning clothes
    (b) Waste treatment
    (c) None
    (d) Both

314. Which micro-organism is widely used in genetic engineering experiments?
    (a) Pseudomonas
    (b) Bacillius subtilis
    (c) Rhizobium
    (d) Escherichia coli

315. In addition to flour, water, salt, etc., bread-making essentially needs one of the following items. Which one?
    (a) Yeast
    (b) Sugar
    (c) Egg
    (d) Colouring agent

316. What does In Vitro Fertilization (IVF) deal with?
  (a) Embryo (b) Egg
  (c) Uterus (d) All

317. What encodes for different proteins in the human body?
  (a) Chromosome (b) Nucleotide
  (c) Virus (d) Cell

318. Which technique is genetic engineering?
  (a) DNA manipulation (b) Gene therapy
  (c) Cloning (d) All

319. Which is considered a cure for cancer?
  (a) Monoclonal antibodies
  (b) Interferon
  (c) Both (d) None

320. Which material is genetically modified or altered for various needs?
  (a) DNA (b) RNA
  (c) Both (d) None

Environment

321. Which invention does not consume any fuel, does not create any pollution, keeps one fit and is inexpensive too?
  (a) Radio (b) Bicycle
  (c) Solar oven (d) Sailship

322. If the global temperature falls by this much degree, an Ice age will engulf the earth. What is the temperature?
    (a) 1 degree C   (b) 10 degree C
    (c) 17 degree C   (d) 4 degree C

323. Which gas plays a decisive role in affecting the climate of the earth?
    (a) Oxygen   (b) Nitrogen
    (c) Carbon dioxide   (d) Hydrogen

324. Which living organism is most affected by acid rains?
    (a) Mammals   (b) Fish
    (c) Birds   (d) Bacteria

325. Supersonic aircraft and rockets cause maximum damage to one thing. What is it?
    (a) Stratosphere   (b) Aurora Borealis
    (c) Ozone layer   (d) Ionosphere

326. Which ecosystem is the oldest of all?
    (a) Coral reefs   (b) Tropical rain forests
    (c) Mangroves   (d) Estuaries

327. India has three types of biomes of the following four. Which is the odd one out?
    (a) Tropical rain forest (b) Savanna
    (c) Temperate grassland   (d) Scrub

328. Which is the scientific name attributed to the earth as a living organism?
   (a) Sita
   (b) Gaia
   (c) Hermes
   (d) Green planet

329. Which living being is a good pollution monitor?
   (a) Mollusc
   (b) Shark
   (c) Armadillo
   (d) Sunflower

330. What is the main agent responsible for thinning of egg shells of birds and in some cases leading to their reproductive failure?
   (a) DDT
   (b) Sulphur dioxide fumes
   (c) Mercury
   (d) Acid rains

331. Which defoliant was used on a mass scale in Vietnam to cause diseases and deaths among humans and animals, apart from destroying trees and plants?
   (a) Agent Red
   (b) Agent Orange
   (c) Both
   (d) None

332. What causes the maximum noise pollution?
   (a) Motor car
   (b) Aircraft take-off
   (c) Pop music
   (d) Railway engine

333. During 1957-58, scientists of different countries joined hands to conduct a worldwide study of the earth and her environment. What was the experiment called?
   (a) Global Research Project
   (b) International Scientific Expedition to Earth.
   (c) World Study of Earth
   (d) International Geophysical Year

Antarctica

334. Where is Antarctica located?
   (a) North Pole   (b) South Pole
   (c) Greenland   (d) Equator

335. Which planet has conditions similar to those present on Antarctica?
   (a) Mercury   (b) Jupiter
   (c) Venus   (d) Mars

336. Which phenomenon does not occur in Antarctica?
   (a) Mirage   (b) Aurora Australis
   (c) Whiteout   (d) Tornado

337. Which living being is not found in Antarctica?
   (a) Leopard seal   (b) King penguin
   (c) Polar bear   (d) Lichen

338. What is the origin of the name 'Antarctica'?
    (a) The Greek name 'Thule'
    (b) The continent Australasia
    (c) The Bear constellation
    (d) An ancient explorer

339. Which description suits Antarctica most?
    (a) Frozen desert   (b) Ice heaven
    (c) Land of penguins   (d) The frozen continent

340. Where was the first Indian station situated in Antarctica?
    (a) Queen Maud Land
    (b) Ross ice shelf
    (c) Adelie Land   (d) Breadmore glacier

341. What is the minimum temperature recorded in Antarctica and where?
    (a) – 88 degree C, Vostok, the Russian station
    (b) – 10 degree C, Vostok, the Russian station
    (c) – 36 degree C, McMurdo Sound, the American station
    (d) – 70 degree C, McMurdo Sound, the American station.

342. Which type of penguin is named after an explorer's wife?
    (a) Gentoo penguin   (b) King penguin
    (c) Adelie penguin   (d) None

343. What is the name of the second Indian station in Antarctica?
    (a) Uttar Gangotri   (b) Paschim Gangotri
    (c) Maitree   (d) Dosti

344. If Antarctica were to melt, by how many metres will the level of seas rise?
    (a) About 100 metres   (b) About 60 metres
    (c) About 160 metres   (d) About 10 metres

345. Antarctica is an uncontaminated and well-preserved source of this. What is it?
    (a) Diamonds   (b) Krill
    (c) Meteorites   (d) Crystals

XII

SCIENCE FOR VILLAGES, INDUSTRY AND WEAPONRY

Villages

346. Which invention will solve the energy crisis of most Indian villages, provided it becomes cheap and more efficient?
    (a) Solar cells   (b) Laser fusion
    (c) Tidal power generator (d) Windmill

347. During this programme, thousands of villages in India were shown TV programmes using an American satellite. What was it called?
    (a) SITE   (b) STEP
    (c) NEXT   (d) INSAT

348. Which species of trees is suitable for cultivation in wastelands?
    (a) Dhaman   (b) Coral Jasmine
    (c) Neem   (d) Baobab

349. Which energy source has been tried on a large scale in rural areas in India?
   (a) Mini nuclear plants   (b) Biogas plants
   (c) Windmills   (d) Mini thermal plants

350. Which communication means should first be improved for rural areas?
   (a) Bicycle   (b) Bullock cart
   (c) Railway lines   (d) Tonga

351. Which species of fast-growing trees is nowadays being planted on a large scale in rural areas for fuel and oil?
   (a) Kevda   (b) Kanju
   (c) Eucalyptus   (d) Asan

352. Which Indian state has the largest area of wasteland?
   (a) Nagaland   (b) Uttaranchal
   (c) Maharashtra   (d) Rajasthan

353. What should be improved so that everybody in rural areas can conserve fuel?
   (a) Stove   (b) Solar dryer
   (c) Chulha   (d) Petromax

354. Which energy source can be easily exploited for generating energy in hilly and rainy areas?
(a) Small dams
(b) Power packs
(c) Solar cells
(d) None

355. Which Indian state has the maximum amount of forest cover area?
(a) West Bengal
(b) Meghalaya
(c) Madhya Pradesh
(d) Orissa

Industry

356. Which industry consumes the largest amount of wood?
(a) Matchwood
(b) Sports goods
(c) Furniture
(d) Paper and pulp

357. What are robots likely to be used for in industries on a large scale?
(a) Keeping an eye on the workers.
(b) Moving products from factory to store.
(c) Giving a helping hand to workers.
(d) Welding.

358. Which mathematical subject is used extensively in industries for quality control of products?
(a) Topology
(b) Statistics
(c) Projective geometry
(d) Mensuration

359. Which subject is likely to revolutionise industries soon?
    (a) Biotechnology
    (b) Laser
    (c) Superconductivity
    (d) Ceramics

360. Which of the following has caused a new type of respiratory disease among workers who handle it in factories?
    (a) Diamond
    (b) Graphite
    (c) Asbestos
    (d) Bakelite

361. Which is the cheapest industrial acid?
    (a) Sulphuric acid
    (b) Hydrochloric acid
    (c) Nitric acid
    (d) Citric acid

362. Which industry can make the earth uninhabitable for life?
    (a) Space industry
    (b) Mining industry
    (c) Shipping industry
    (d) Nuclear industry

363. Which is the biggest industry in the world?
    (a) Oil
    (b) Chemicals
    (c) Weapon
    (d) Space

364. Which industry creates maximum environmental pollution?
    (a) Petrochemical
    (b) Electronic
    (c) Aircraft
    (d) Paper

365. Which chemical industry provides a wider range of products than any other?
    (a) Polymer   (b) Pharmaceutical
    (c) Agrochemical   (d) Heavy chemical

Weaponry

366. Where was the first atom bomb tested?
    (a) Bikini islands   (b) Los Alamos
    (c) Ural mountains   (d) Alamogordo

367. Which bomb only harms life but leaves man-made objects unaffected?
    (a) Hydrogen bomb   (b) Neutron bomb
    (c) Atom bomb   (d) None

368. Which weapon will always be on wheels shuttling from one place to another?
    (a) Cruise missile   (b) MX missile
    (c) Satellite-killer
    (d) Intercontinental ballisticmissile

369. Which is India's anti-tank missile?
    (a) Trishul   (b) Pinaka
    (c) Nag   (d) Saras

370. Which is India's remotely piloted vehicle used for battlefield surveillance and reconnaissance?
    (a) Nag
    (b) Panchendriya
    (c) Falcon
    (d) Anupam

371. Which missile is launched like a rocket but homes in on its target like an aircraft?
    (a) Submarine launched ballistic missile
    (b) Cruise missile
    (c) Exocet missile
    (d) None

372. Which is the most expensive weaponry programme devised to date?
    (a) ICBM
    (b) Star Wars
    (c) SLBM
    (d) Polaris

373. Where have nuclear bomb shelters been built?
    (a) USA
    (b) UK
    (c) Russia.
    (d) Switzerland

374. Which space vehicle could be used as a weapon during war?
    (a) Landsat
    (b) Space shuttle
    (c) Spy satellite
    (d) Pioneer-10

375. Which newly invented device is likely to be employed in a hand-to-hand combat?
    (a) Computer
    (b) Robot
    (c) Remote sensing satellite
    (d) None

376. Which rays is used for 'seeing' during night?
   (a) Ultraviolet
   (b) X-ray
   (c) Laser
   (d) Infrared

377. What was the code name of the first atom bomb that was dropped over Japan?
   (a) Little Boy
   (b) Bad Luck
   (c) Goodbye
   (d) Baby

378. Which is India's first indigenously built fighter plane?
   (a) Gnat
   (b) Mig-21
   (c) LCA
   (d) HF-24

379. Which is India's surface-to-air missile with multiple target-handling capability?
   (a) Agni
   (b) Trishul
   (c) Prithvi
   (d) Akash

XIII

DATES & QUOTES

Dates

380. A person who is against technology is often called a 'Luddite'. This term has its origin in riots when some unemployed youth tried to destroy machines in the United Kingdom. When did these riots occur?
    (a) 1800
    (b) 1890
    (c) 1870
    (d) 1812

381. When did Edward Jenner discover the smallpox vaccine?
    (a) 1897
    (b) 1567
    (c) 1689
    (d) 1796

382. When did John Dalton's *New System of Chemical Philosophy*, in which he gave his atomic theory, appear?
    (a) 1810
    (b) 1934
    (c) 1876
    (d) 1890

383. When did James Watt invent the steam engine?
    (a) 1889   (b) 1679
    (c) 1907   (d) 1765

384. When did the Montgolfier brothers successfully go
    up in the air in a balloon?
    (a) 1790   (b) 1890
    (c) 1783   (d) 1900

385. When did Carl Linnaeus's *Systema Naturae*, in
    which he gave the classification of animals, plants
    and minerals appear?
    (a) 1230   (b) 1580
    (c) 1409   (d) 1768

386. It is said that for about 400 years India was the centre
    of mathematics in the world. When did India's
    supremacy in mathematics begin?
    (a) A.D. 500   (b) A.D. 800
    (c) A. D. 400   (d) 200 B.C.

387. When was Isaac Newton's monumental work
    Principia Mathematica published?
    (a) 1579   (b) 1687
    (c) 1587   (d) 1479

388. When was Giordano Bruno burnt at stake for having supported scientific investigations?
  (a) 1200   (b) 1500
  (c) 1600   (d) 1700

389. When was Nicolaus Copernicus's book *De Revolutionibus Orbium Coelestium*, which created a revolution in astronomy by claiming the sun to be the centre of the universe, published?
  (a) 1543   (b) 1657
  (c) 1190   (d) None

390. When did the famous bird-watcher Salim Ali's interesting findings about the life of weaver-birds appear?
  (a) 1970   (b) 1960
  (c) 1930   (d) 1950

391. When did John Baird give the first live demonstration of television?
  (a) 1906   (b) 1926
  (c) 1946   (d) 1966

392. When was the Human Genome Project started?
  (a) 1968   (b) 1988
  (c) 1978   (d) 1998

393. It is said that with the rise of the Gupta dynasty in India, considerable mathematical, technological and medical advancements were made in the country. When did the Gupta dynasty begin?
   (a) A.D. 579
   (b) A.D. 320
   (c) 135 B.C.
   (d) A.D. 110

394. When did S. N. Bose, an eminent Indian physicist, give the idea of 'Boson' – a type of elementary particle?
   (a) 1978
   (b) 1924
   (c) 1960
   (d) 1908

Quotations

395. Who said, 'There is no royal road to geometry'?
   (a) Appollonius
   (b) Anaximander
   (c) Pythagoras
   (d) Euclid

396. Who said, 'Give me but one firm spot on which to stand, and I will move the earth'?
   (a) Aristotle
   (b) Archimedes
   (c) Aristarchus
   (d) Apollonius

397. Who said, 'Truly man is king of beasts for his brutality exceeds theirs'?
   (a) Aristotle
   (b) Charles Darwin
   (c) Leonardo da Vinci
   (d) Alfred Wallace

398. Who said, 'I think, therefore I am'?
    (a) G. W. Leibniz   (b) Plato
    (c) Rene Descartes   (d) Immanuel Kant

399. Who said, 'Taking an active part in the solutions of
     the problems of peace is a moral duty which no
     conscientious man can shirk'?
    (a) Freeman Dyson   (b) Albert Einstein
    (c) Francis Crick   (d) Linus Pauling

400. Who remarked, 'I do not know what I may appear
     to the world, but to myself I seem to have been only
     a boy playing on the sea-shore, and diverting myself
     in now and then finding a smoother pebble or a pret
     tier she ll than ordinary, whilst the great ocean of
     truth lay all undiscovered before me'?
    (a) Isaac Newton   (b) Johannes Kepler
    (c) Albert Einstein   (d) C. V. Raman

401. Which scientist said, 'Science is a long history of
     learning how not to fool ourselves'?
    (a) Richard Feynman   (b) Carl Sagan
    (c) Max Planck   (d) Peter Medawar

402. Who said, 'I hate doubt, and yet I am certain that
     doubt is the only way to approach anything worth
     believing in'?
    (a) J.B.S. Haldane   (b) Edward Teller
    (c) Samuel Ting   (d) Blaise Pascal

403. Who said, 'It was almost as incredible as if you fired a 15 inch shell at a tissue paper and it bounced back and hit you'?
(a) Ernest Rutherford   (b) Niels Bohr
(c) Edward Teller   (d) Otto Hahn

404. Who said, 'Science has promised us truth..... It has never promised us either peace or happiness'?
(a) George Bernard Shaw
(b) Gustave le Bon
(c) Leo Tolstoy   (d) Richard Feynman

405. Which writer said, 'Science says the first word on everything and the last word on nothing'?
(a) George Orwell   (b) Victor Hugo
(c) Aldous Huxley   (d) Jules Verne

406. Which politician and statesman said, 'Science does not simply sit down and pray for things to happen but seeks to find out why things happen'?
(a) M. K. Gandhi   (b) B. G. Tilak
(c) Subhash Chandra Bose
(d) Jawahar Lal Nehru

407. Which philosopher of science said, 'What science has to teach us ..... is not its techniques but its spirit : the irrestible need to explore'?
(a) A. N. Whitehead   (b) J. D. Bernal
(c) Ludwig Wittgenstein   (d) Jacob Bronowski

XIV
BOOKS AND INSTITUTES

Books

408. Which book brought public attention to the harmful effects of DDT in the USA and created a worldwide stir?
    (a) *Silent Spring*
    (b) *Life on Earth*
    (c) *Nature Watch*
    (d) *The Living Planet*

409. Which book gave a new insight into the unconscious mind?
    (a) *Science and Human Behaviour*
    (b) *Objective Knowledge*
    (c) *The Life of the Mind*
    (d) *The Interpretation of Dreams*

410. Which is the first science book to be published in the world?
    (a) Aristotle's *Organon*
    (b) Hippocrates' *Aphorisms*
    (c) Pliny's *Natural History*
    (d) Archimedes' *On the Sphere and Cylinder*

411. Who is the author of the scientific classic *On the Structure of the Human Body*?
   (a) Galen
   (b) Andreas Vesalius
   (c) Aristotle
   (d) Avicenna

412. Which popular literary book's plot is basically a mathematical game and contains a lot of unexplained science?
   (a) *Alice in Wonderland*
   (b) *Gulliver's Travels*
   (c) *Frankenstein*
   (d) *A Christmas Carol*

413. Who wrote *Brihatsamhita*, a master collection of scientific information on diverse subjects?
   (a) Varahamihira
   (b) Charaka
   (c) Nagarjuna
   (d) Kanada

414. Which classic was written by an astronomer-king?
   (a) *Dialogue on the Two Chief World Systems*
   (b) *Almagest*
   (c) *Selenographia*
   (d) *Sidereus Nuncius*

415. Who wrote *Leelavati*, a classic work on algebra?
   (a) Brahmagupta
   (b) Diophantus
   (c) Bhaskara
   (d) Aryabhata

416. Which book introduced Hindu numbers and
mathematics to Europe?
(a) *Liber Abcai*
(b) *Hisab al-jabr wa-al-muqabalah*
(c) *Natural Questions*   (d) *Opus Majus*

417. Which book released chemistry from medical men
and made its author the founder of modern chemistry?
(a) *Chemistry Applied to Medical Arts*
(b) *The Sceptical Chemist*
(c) *Introduction to Natural Philosophy*
(d) *Elementary Treatise on Chemistry*

International Institutes

418. Where is the oldest observatory in the world situated?
(a) Copenhagen, Denmark
(b) Greenwich, UK
(c) Chomsongdae, South Korea
(d) Mount Hopkins, USA

419. Which is the science body that coordinates efforts
in different branches of science and its applications
at international level, among other things?
(a) INSA   (b) ICSU
(c) AAAS   (d) COSPAR

420. Where are the headquarters of the World Wide
Fund for Nature located?
(a) Mumbai, India   (b) Los Angeles, USA
(c) New Jersey, Channel Islands
(d) Gland, Switzerland

421. Which astronomical observatory's longitude is considered to be zero?
(a) Paris Observatory, France
(b) Royal Observatory, Greenwich, UK
(c) Madras Observatory, India
(d) Pulkova Observatory, Russia

422. Where are the headquarters of the World Health
Organisation located?
(a) Rome, Italy
(b) Manila, Philippines
(c) Geneva, Switzerland
(d) Pittsburgh, USA

423. Which is the science body whose aim is
encouragement of science and technology in
developing countries?
(a) IAU   (b) COSTED
(c) ISCA   (d) None

424. Where is the International Atomic Energy Agency,
the major body to promote peaceful uses of nuclear
energy and keep a watch on nuclear installations,
located?
(a) Karachi, Pakistan   (b) Illinois, USA
(c) Vienna, Austria   (d) Paris, France

425. Which is the only flying observatory in the world?
(a) Kuiper Airborne Laboratory
(b) Spacelab
(c) Jet Propulsion Laboratory
(d) Skylab

426. Which is the oldest science museum in the world?
(a) Science Museum, UK
(b) American Museum of Natural Histroy, USA
(c) National Museum of Natural History, India
(d) National Museum of Man, Canada

427. Where are the headquarters of the UNESCO located?
(a) Paris, France   (b) Moscow, Russia
(c) Washington, USA   (d) Canberra, Australia

428. Which international body awards the Kalinga Prize
for popularisation of science?
(a) UNESCO   (b) UN
(c) WWF   (d) UNDP

429. Where are the headquarters of the Food and Agriculture Organisation located?
(a) Paris, France
(b) Colombo, Sri Lanka
(c) Tokyo, Japan
(d) Rome, Italy

430. Where is the Royal Society – the most prestigious science body today – located?
(a) Glasgow, UK
(b) New York, USA
(c) London, UK
(d) Munich, Germany

431. Clocks the world over are set according to the time indicated by this astronomical observatory. Which is it?
(a) U. S. Naval Observatory, Washington.
(b) Royal Greenwich Observatory, UK
(c) Royal Observatory, Pittsburgh, UK
(d) Harvard Observatory, UK

432. Where are the headquarters of the World Meteorological Organisation located?
(a) Los Angeles, USA
(b) Geneva, Switzerland
(c) New Delhi, India
(d) London, UK

433. Which international body has been set up to maintain the earth's biosphere?
(a) IUCN
(b) UNESCO
(c) WWF
(d) UNEF

XV

AUTHORS, ASTRONOMERS AND CONSERVATIONISTS

Scientists Who Write

434. Who is the most popular writer on mathematical puzzles, recreations and diversions?
    (a) Warren Weaver   (b) Martin Gardner
    (c) H. E. Dudeney   (d) E. T. Bell

435. Who is the author of the bestseller *The Dragons of Eden*?
    (a) Douglas Adams   (b) Carl Sagan
    (c) Alvin Toffler   (d) Tom Wolfe

436. Who are the authors of the most infamous book *The Secret Life of Plants*?
    (a) Max Flint and Otto O. Binder
    (b) Edward A. Feigenbaum and Pamela McCorduck
    (c) Heather Couper and Nigel Henbest
    (d) Peter Tompkins and Christopher Bird

437. Who is the author of the prophetic book *Profiles of the Future*?
   (a) Arthur C. Clarke   (b) Alvin Toffler
   (c) Isaac Asimov   (d) J. G. Crowther

438. Who wrote the bestseller *The Selfish Gene*?
   (a) Paul Harrison   (b) James Watson
   (c) Oliver Sacks   (d) Richard Dawkins

439. Who wrote the thought-provoking book *The Demon-Haunted World* which made a strong plea for popularising science?
   (a) Stephen Jay Gould   (b) Carl Sagan
   (c) V. S. Venkatavardan
   (d) Stephen Hawking

440. Who made the classic TV serial *The Ascent of Man* concerning the evolution of science and technology?
   (a) Jacob Bronowski   (b) Kenneth Clark
   (c) Joseph Needham   (d) Colin A. Ronan

441. Who are the authors of the voluminous *Handbook of Birds of India and Pakistan*?
   (a) Salim Ali and S. Dillon Ripley
   (b) Jafar Futehally and Salim Ali
   (c) E. P. Gee and T. J. Roberts
   (d) Ranjit Lal

442. Who wrote the classic *Phantoms in the Brain*
     based on his own findings on the brain-body rela-
     tionships?
     (a) V.S.Ramachandra   (b) Claude Bernard
     (c) John Maddox   (d) Peter Medawar

443. Who is famous for his writings on astronomy and
     night-sky watching?
     (a) Nigel Henbest   (b) James Cornell
     (c) Patrick Moore   (d) Lief J. Robinson

444. Who wrote *The Tao of Physics* which gave for the
     first time parallels between modern physics and
     mysticism?
     (a) E.C.G. Surarshan   (b) Fritjof Capra
     (c) John Wheeler   (d) David Bohm

445. Who wrote *The Road Ahead* which talked about
     the way the internet will revolutionise our lives?
     (a) Raj Reddy   (b) Bill Gates
     (c) Claude Shannon   (d) Steve Jobs

446. Who wrote the international bestseller *A Brief
     History of Time* throwing light on the origin of the
     universe?
     (a) Carl Sagan   (b) Roger Penrose
     (c) J.V.Narlikar   (d) Stephen Hawking

447. Whose autobiography is *Wings of Fire*?
 - (a) Satish Dhawan
 - (b) Vikram Sarabhai
 - (c) A. P. J. Kalam
 - (d) U. R. Rao

448. Who is the biggest populariser of evolutionary biology in the recent times?
 - (a) Carl Sagan
 - (b) David Attenborough
 - (c) D. Balasubrimanian
 - (d) Stephen Jay Gould

Watchers of the Sky

449. Who first made an estimate of the distance between the earth and the sun?
 - (a) Pythagoras
 - (b) Aristarchus
 - (c) Johannes Kepler
 - (d) Edmund Halley

450. Who discovered the planet Pluto?
 - (a) Clyde Tombaugh
 - (b) John Herschel
 - (c) Percival Lowell
 - (d) William Herschel

451. Who first discovered 'sunspots' – the black spots – on the surface of the sun?
 - (a) J. Fabricius
 - (b) John Herschel
 - (c) William Herschel
 - (d) Hipparchus

452. Who was the first to discover radio emissions from the sun?
   (a) J. R. Mayer
   (b) J. S. Hey
   (c) J. Van Allen
   (d) J. Janssen

453. Who discovered the rotation of the sun?
   (a) Galileo Galilei
   (b) G. D. Cassani
   (c) Nicolaus Copernicus
   (d) Fred Hoyle

454. Who discovered the rings of the planet Uranus?
   (a) W. H. Pickering
   (b) J. C. Bhattacharya
   (c) M.K.V. Bappu
   (d) Voyager-II

455. Who discovered the 1987 A supernova in the Large Magellanic Cloud?
   (a) Albert Jones
   (b) Ian Shelton
   (c) Rob McNaught
   (d) M. K.V. Bappu

456. Who was the first to give the precise position of the planet Neptune before its discovery?
   (a) John C. Adams
   (b) U. J. J. Le Verrier
   (c) Both
   (d) None

457. Who was the first to give the precise position of the planet Pluto before its discovery?
   (a) W. H. Pickering
   (b) V. B. Ketkar
   (c) Clyde Tombaugh
   (d) F. L. Whipple

458. Who discovered the satellite of the planet Pluto?
    (a) James W. Christy   (b) Charles Kowal
    (c) Gerard Kuiper   (d) D. P. Todd

459. Which important American astronomical observatory is named after this astronomer?
    (a) George Hale   (b) William Herschel
    (c) Tycho Brahe   (d) Asaph Hall

460. Who has discovered the largest number of comets?
    (a) Edmund Halley   (b) V. Clube
    (c) J. L. Pons   (d) David Gill

461. Which group of astronomical objects is known after the name of this astronomer?
    (a) Ferdinand Magellan
    (b) Charles Messier
    (c) Edwin Hubble   (d) Edmund Halley

462. Who discovered Chiron, with its orbit between those of Saturn and Uranus?
    (a) Harlow Shapley   (b) Charles Kowal
    (c) K. Hirayama   (d) Thomas Gehrels

463. Who obtained the first solar spectrum?
    (a) Aristotle   (b) Gustav Kirchhoff
    (c) Joseph von Fraunhofer
    (d) Isaac Newton

464. Who claimed that life was brought to earth on a comet?
   (a) Fred Whipple   (b) Fred Hoyle
   (c) Hermann Bondi
   (d) Chandra Wickramasinghe

465. Who firmly believed in aliens visiting the earth?
   (a) Carl Sagan   (b) J. Allen Hynek
   (c) Fred Hoyle   (d) James Jeans

466. Who discovered the satellites of Jupiter ?
   (a) Fred Hoyle   (b) S.Chandrasekhar
   (c) Tycho Brahe   (d) Galileo Galilei

Conservationists

467. Who is mainly responsible for saving the Peregrine falcon from extinction?
   (a) Thomas C. Cade   (b) George Schaller
   (c) Stuart Baker   (d) Salim Ali

468. Which naturalist was murdered because of her efforts to save gorillas?
   (a) Mariam Rothschild   (b) Agnes Clark
   (c) Dian Fossey   (d) Neville Coleman

469. Who wanted to build a zoo from his childhood and did own a special type of zoo?
    (a) Konrad Lorenz   (b) Gerald Durrell
    (c) W. H. Thoreau   (d) None

470. Who fought a battle against the release of genetically manipulated bacteria into the environment in the USA?
    (a) Stanley Cohen   (b) Francis Crick
    (c) Barbara Maclintock
    (d) Jeremy Rifkin

471. Who has saved the endangered bird Cahow from extinction?
    (a) Louis L. Mowbary   (b) Paul Spitzer
    (c) David Wingate   (d) Richard Pough

472. Who started the 'Chipko' movement in Uttar Pradesh to save forests from timber contractors?
    (a) Chandi Prasad Bhatt
    (b) Bunker Roy
    (c) Sunder Lal Bahuguna
    (d) Kamala Choudhary

473. Who was murdered for lobbying against nuclear power plants and weapons?
    (a) Roselie Bartell   (b) Barry Mathews
    (c) Hilda Murrell   (d) John Taylor

474. Where did the Green Party, a party that fights at political level for ecology and related issues, origi nate in?
    (a) United Kingdom   (b) Italy
    (c) Germany   (d) USA

475. Who is the founder of the 'Beauty Without Cruelty' society?
    (a) Muriel Dowding   (b) Mariam Rothschild
    (c) Barbara Ward   (D) Margaret Mead

476. Which is the Indian tribe that reveres animal life and is ready to sacrifice life for saving it?
    (a) Todas   (b) Bhils
    (c) Bishnois   (d) Santhals

XVI

MISCELLANY

Science Affects Society

477. Which invention created the conditions for the Civil War in the USA?
(a) Cotton gin
(b) Railways
(c) Telephone
(d) Street light

478. When this invention arrived on the scene, people heaved a sigh of relief thinking that it would free them of pollution. But, today it is creating massive pollution of a different kind. What is it?
(a) Aeroplane
(b) Computer
(c) Motor car
(d) Tram

479. Which invention was the first to be of direct use to women, in fact it became 'a woman's best friend'?
(a) Refrigerator
(b) Sewing machine
(c) Knitting machine
(d) Typewriter

480. Which invention has allowed us to see that our planet is an 'Oasis in space' whose safety and unity is in our hands?
    (a) Telescope
    (b) Rocket
    (c) Satellite
    (d) None

481. Which invention has killed the imagination of people and caused considerable eye problems?
    (a) Printed books
    (b) Television
    (c) Computer
    (d) Cinema

482. Which invention had created a scare, especially among ladies, when it was announced in the daily press?
    (a) X-rays
    (b) Contraceptives
    (c) Lipstick
    (d) Safety pin

483. Which invention has made the world sit on our table?
    (a) Television
    (b) Radio
    (c) Telephone
    (d) Tape recorder

484. Which invention was the first to assist the police in catching an absconding criminal?
    (a) Microscope
    (b) Television
    (c) Railways
    (d) Wireless radio

485. Which invention is considered to have built America?
    (a) Motor car
    (b) Television
    (c) Dynamite
    (d) Railways

486. Who coined the term 'future shock'–implying people have to adjust to fast changing environment brought in by new discoveries and inventions?
    (a) Lewis Thomas
    (b) B. F. Skinner
    (c) Alvin Toffler
    (d) Kenneth Clark

Other Than Science

487. Which astronomer had an artificial nose?
    (a) Tycho Brahe
    (b) Hipparchus
    (c) Johann Kepler
    (d) Percival Lowell

488. Who is more renowned for his poetry than his studies in mathematics or astronomy?
    (a) Roger Bacon
    (b) George Fitzgerald
    (c) Omar Khayyam
    (d) Francesco Grimaldi

489. Which scientist was guillotined for reasons other than scientific?
    (a) Giordano Bruno
    (b) Antoine Lavoisier
    (c) Tycho Brahe
    (d) Galileo Galilei

490. Who is more renowned for his textbooks on chemistry rather than research in chemistry?
   - (a) Henry Cavendish
   - (b) Joseph Black
   - (c) P. C. Ray
   - (d) Samuel Glasstone

491. Who is more renowned for his thoughts on social philosophy rather than his researches in chemistry?
   - (a) Giulio Natta
   - (b) Linus Pauling
   - (c) Micheal Polanyi
   - (d) George Porter

492. Who is known as the 'Wizard of Menlo Park'?
   - (a) George Westinghouse
   - (b) Thomas Alva Edison
   - (c) John Fleming
   - (d) Leonardo da Vinci

493. Who was called Charles Darwin's 'bulldog'?
   - (a) Herbert Spencer
   - (b) T. H. Huxley
   - (c) T. H. Morgan
   - (d) G. G. Simpson

494. Who is more renowned as an excellent painter of birds rather than a naturalist?
   - (a) John James Audubon
   - (b) Salim Ali
   - (c) S. Dillon Ripley
   - (d) Charles Beebe

495. Which famous hoax concerns human-ape fossils?
   - (a) Piltdown hoax
   - (b) Great Moon hoax
   - (c) Fitzroy hoax
   - (d) Schiaparelli hoax

General

496. Where has the biggest nuclear reactor accident taken place in the world?
    - (a) Chernobyl
    - (b) Three Mile Islands
    - (c) Mururoa
    - (d) Berkeley

497. Where was a big cloud of methyl isocyanate released by a chemical factory killing a large number of persons?
    - (a) Bhopal, India
    - (b) Venice, Italy
    - (c) Leningrad, Russia.
    - (d) Bonn, Germany

498. Which is considered to be the most respected and the oldest science journal in the world?
    - (a) Science
    - (b) Nature
    - (c) Science and Culture
    - (d) Current Science

499. Which is the major subject area in science that has emerged in recent times?
    - (a) Ethnology
    - (b) Chaos
    - (c) Entropy
    - (d) Environment

500. Which is the region where ships and aircraft vanish without trace?
    - (a) Bering strait
    - (b) Panama canal
    - (c) Dead sea
    - (d) Bermuda triangle

501. It is claimed that there was once another continent with a prospering and rich civilisation. Where is that continent believed to have been present?
    (a) Pacific ocean   (b) Indian ocean
    (c) Atlantic ocean   (d) Red sea

502. Which is the new emerging field in the area of biology?
    (a) Bioinformatics   (b) Evolutionary biology
    (c) Biotechnology   (d) Biophysics

503. Which invention triggered off the era of automation?
    (a) Steam engine   (b) Servomechanism
    (c) Valve   (d) All

504. What is the project Cyclops concerned with?
    (a) Life on sea-bed   (b) Lunar colonies
    (c) Extraterrestria Intelligence
    (d) Robot spacecraft

505. Who are the ultimate rulers of earth?
    (a) Humans   (b) Robots
    (c) Computers   (d) Microbes

506. Who founded the international science journal *Nature*?
    (a) Alexander Bell   (b) Fred Hoyle
    (c) Norman Lockyer   (d) J. G. Crowther

507. What is the missing word in this limerick?
There was a young girl called
Miss Bright
Who could travel much
faster than light
    She departed one day
The _____ way
And came back the previous night.
(a) Aristotlien   (b) Galilean
(c) Newtonian   (d) Einsteinian

508. What causes Severe Acute Respiratory Syndrome
(SARS)?
(a) Bacteria   (b) Virus
(c) Oncogene   (d) All

509. Which GM (Genetically Modified) crop recently
came in the news when it was cultivated illegally in
India?
(a) Rice   (b) Cotton
(c) Wheat   (d) Jute

510. Which is presently a controversial subject in the field
of genetic engineering?
(a) Stem cell research   (b) Gene therapy
(c) Genetically Modified food
(d) All

511. What is the name of the International Space Station presently being assembled in space?
    (a) Enterprise   (b) Freedom
    (c) Ulysses   (d) Endeavour

512. The space telescope presently orbiting the earth is named in honour of this astronomer. Who is he?
    (a) Edwin P. Hubble   (b) Harlow Shapley
    (c) Otto Struve   (d) Bernard Lowell

Q. 513 It is neither a passage to a temple nor a hall of a fort. It is meant for performing scientific observations. What is it and what is its purpose?

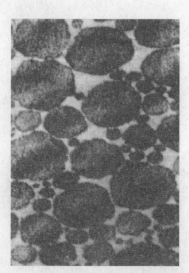

Q. 514 An electron microscopic view of a part of the body of all mammals. What is it?

Q. 515 It is the conspicuous feature of one of the planets. What is the feature called? Which is that planet?

Q. 516 What is this camera-like object? It is certainly not a camera. What is it, then?

Q. 517 What is this round object that is being carefully handled? What was its purpose?

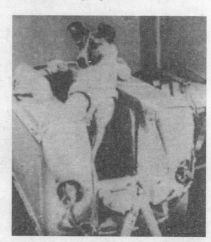

Q. 518 This is a very important dog. What is its name? What important thing did it do?

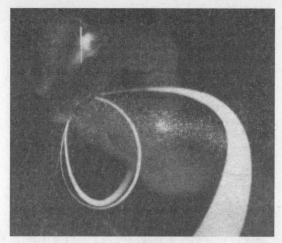

Q. 519 Can a ray of light be handled in this manner? No. But, then, what is responsible for making it do so? What are its applications?

Q. 520 This equipment has considerable antique value. What is it?

Q. 521 Identify this object. What was its purpose?

Q. 522 What is this object and its purpose?

Q. 523 What type of clouds are hovering around Eiffel Tower?

Q .524 What is this object? What is its most special quality?

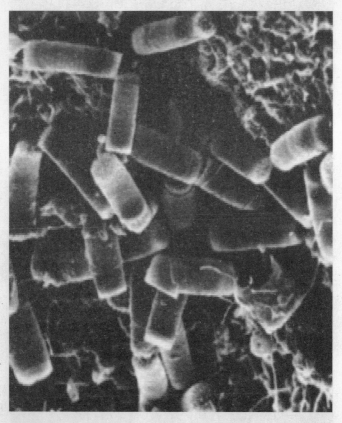

Q. 525 These are found in large numbers in seas and rivers. What are they? What is their economic utility

ANSWERS

1.(d)
2.(c)
3.(b)
4.(d)
5.(a)
6.(d)
7.(a)
8.(c)
9.(b)
10.(a)
11.(a)
12.(c)
13.(a)
14.(a)
15.(c)
16.(d)
17.(d)
18.(b)
19.(c) Leibniz built a calculator
20.(a)
21.(a) and (b)
22.(b)
23.(d)
24.(d)
25.(b)
26.(a)
27.(a)
28.(d)
29.(a)
30.(d)
31.(b)
32.(a)

33.(c)
34.(c)
35.(c)
36.(a)
37.(a)
38.(b)
39.(c)
40.(a)
41.(a)
42.(c)
43.(a)
44.(d)
45.(b)
46.(a)
47.(a) Stephenson built the first workable railway engine and commercialised rail travel.
48.(c)
49.(b) Galileo rebuilt Lippershey's invention and trained telescope on the night sky.
50.(b)
51.(b)
52.(b)
53.(b)
54.(d) Quite likely, an Indian accountant.

55.(b)
56.(b)
57.(b)
58.(a)
59.(a)
60.(b)
61.(a)
62.(a)
63.(b)
65.(c)
66.(a)
67.(c)
68.(d)
69.(a)
70.(b)
71.(d)
72.(c)
73.(c)
74.(c)
75.(a)
76.(b)
77.(c)
78.(d)
79.(c)
80.(b)
81.(a)
82.(a)
83.(b)
84.(b)
85.(a)
86.(b)
87.(c)
88.(d)

89.(a)
90.(a)
91.(a)
92.(a)
93.(d)
94.(c)
95.(c)
96.(a)
97.(a)
98.(a)
99.(b)
100.(a)
101.(c)
102.(c)
103.(d)
104.(d)
105.(d)
106.(c)
107.b)
108.(c)
109.(b)
110.(b)
111.(d)
112.(c)
113.(d)
114.(c)
115.(d)
116.(a)
117.(d)
118.(b)
119.(d)
120.(b)
121.(a)
122.(a)
123.(d)
124.(c)

125.(c)
126.(b) They are cooler regions on the surface of the sun.
127.(b)
128.(d)
129.(d)
130.(a)
131.(a)
132.(c)
133.(c)
134.(c)
135.(c)
136.(c)
137.(c)
138.(a)
139.(d)
140.(a)
141.(b)
142.(c)
143.(b)
144.(b)
145.(d)
146.(c)
147.(d)
148.(a)
149.(c)
150.(b)
151.(c)
152.(a)
153.(a)
154.(b)
155.(c)
156.(a)
157.(d)

158.(a)
159.(c)
160.(c)
161.(d)
162.(d)
163.(b)
164.(d)
165.(b)
166.(b)
167.(b)
168.(c)
169.(c)
170.(b)
171.(a)
172.(b)
173.(a)
174.(b)
175.(a)
176.(d)
177.(b)
178.(a)
179.(a)
180.(c)
181.(c)
182.(a)
183.(a)
184.(d)
185.(d)
186.(c)
187.(b)
188.(b)
189.(d)
190.(c)
191.(c)
192.(b)
193.(a)

194.(c)
195.(b)
196.(a)
197.(d)
198.(c)
199.(c)
200.(b)
201.(d)
202.(a)
203.(b)
204.(a)
205.(a)
206.(a)
207.(c)
208.(b)
209.(b)
210.(c)
211.(a)
212.(c)
213.(a)
214.(b)
215.(c)
216.(c)
217.(a)
218.(b)
219.(a)
220.(d)
221.(c)
222.(d)
223.(a)
224.(b)
225.(d)
226.(b)
227.(b)
228.(a)
229.(a)

230.(c)
231.(c)
232.(d)
233.(a)
234.(b)
235.(a)
236.(b)
237.(d)
238.(b)
239.(c)
240.(b)
241.(a)
242.(b)
243.(b)
244.(b)
245.(a)
246.(c)
247.(b)
248.(c)
249.(a)
250.(b)
251.(a)
252.(a)
253.(b)
254.(c)
255.(b)
256.(c)
257.(c)
258.(b)
259.(b)
260.(d)
261.(c)
262.(a)
263.(b)
264.(a)
265.(b)

266.(c)
267.(b)
268.(c)
269.(b)
270.(b)
271.(a)
272.(a)
273.(b)
274. Maria Goeppart-
        Mayer.
275. M.Visvesvaraya
276. William Shockley
277. Har Gobind
        Khorana
278. Charles Goodyear
279. Jagadish Chandra
        Bose
280. Max Planck
281. C.R.Rao
282.Valentina
        Tereshkova
283. A.P.J.Kalam
284. Arno Penzias
     and R.W.Wilson
285. Hans Krebs
286.(a)
287.(d)
288.(c)
289.(a)
290.(a)
291.(d)
292.(c)
293.(a)
294.(a)
295.(a)
296.(c)

297.(a)
298.(d)
299.(a)
300.(d)
301.(a)
302.(d)
303.(d)
304.(c)
305.(a)
306.(b)
307.(a)
308.(a)
309.(b)
310.(d)
311.(b)
312.(a)
313.(b)
314.(d)
315.(a)
316.(d)
317.(b)
318.(d)
319.(b)
320.(a)
321.(b)
322.(d)
323.(c)
324.(b)
325.(c)
326.(a)
327.(d)
328.(b)
329.(a)
330.(a)
331.(b)
332.(b)

333.(d)
334.(b)
335.(d)
336.(d)
337.(c)
338.(c)
339.(a)
340.(a)
341.(a)
342.(c)
343.(c)
344.(b)
345.(c)
346.(a)
347.(a) Satellite Instruction Television Experiment.
348.(c)
349.(b)
350.(b)
351.(c)
352.(d)
353.(c)
354.(a)
355.(c) The former Madhya Pradesh
356.(d)
357.(d)
358.(b)
359.(a)
360.(c)
361.(b)
362.(d)
363.(a)

364.(a)
365.(a)
366.(d)
367.(b)
368.(b)
369.(c)
370.(c)
371.(b)
372.(b)
373.(d)
374.(b)
375.(b)
376.(d)
377.(a)
378.(d)
379.(d)
380.(d)
381.(d)
382.(a)
383.(d)
384.(c)
385.(d)
386.(a)
387.(a)
388.(c)
389.(a)
390.(c)
391.(b)
392.(b)
393.(b)
394.(b)
395.(d)
396.(b)
397.(c)
398.(c)
399.(b)

400.(a)
401.(a)
402.(b)
403.(a) On the discover of the central heavy nucleus of atom.
404.(b)
405.(b)
406.(d)
407.(d)
408.(a)
409.(d)
410.(c)
411.(b)
412.(a)
413.(a)
414.(b)
415.(c)
416.(a)
417.(b)
418.(c)
419.(b)
420.(d)
421.(b)
422.(c)
423.(b)
424.(c)
425.(a)
426.(a)
427.(a)
428.(a)
429.(d)
430.(c)
431.(b)
432.(b)

433.(a)
434.(b)
435.(b)
436.(d)
437.(a)
438.(d)
439.(b)
440.(a)
441.(a)
442.(a)
443.(c)
444.(b)
445.(b)
446.(d)
447.(c)
448.(d)
449.(b)
450.(a)
451.(a)
452.(b)
453.(a)
454.(b)
455.(b)
456.(c)
457.(b)
458.(a)
459.(a)
460.(c)
461.(b)
462.(b)
463.(d)
464.(b) and (d)
465.(b)
466.(d)
467.(a)
468.(c)

469.(b)
470.(d)
471.(c)
472.(a) and (c)
473.(c)
474.(c)
475.(a)
476.(c)
477.(a)
478.(c)
479.(b)
480.(b)
481.(b)
482.(a)
483.(c)
484.(d)
485.(c)
486.(c)
487.(a)
488.(c)
489.(b)
490.(d)
491.(c)
492.(b)
493.(b)
494.(a)
495.(a)
496.(a)
497.(a)
498.(b)
499.(b)
500.(d)
501.(c)
502.(a)
503.(b)
504.(c)

505.(d)   508.(b)   511.(b)
506.(c)   509.(b)   512.(a)
507.(d)   510.(d)

513. Ram Yantra of Jantar Mantar, New Delhi. It was used for determining the positions of stars and planets.

514. Collagen. It is a fibrous protein found in large quantities in the connective tissues of skin, tendons and bone.

515. Olympus Mons, the great volcano on Mars.

516. The first commercial telephone developed by Alexander Bell in 1877.

517. The round object is LAGEOS – Laser Geodynamics Satellite. This satellite made accurate observations of earth's crustal and rotational motions.

518. Laika. It is the first living being to enter space.

519. Light is traveling through an 'optical fibre'. It is now being used in communication, computer and medical equipment.

520. G.Marconi's first transmitter used in his earliest experiments on radio waves in 1894 in Italy.

521. Venus-10 space probe. It studied the surface and environment of the planet Venus.

522. Chickenmesh antenna. During the SITE experiment in 1976, it was installed in thousands in rural areas to bring TV programmes to villagers in some parts of India.

523. Cirrus.

524. The sun-facing side of the earth. It evolved intelligent life.

525. Diatoms – deposits of kieselguhr and oil.

SCORE YOURSELF

Count the correct answers you have given and mark yourself as follows:

Average: if 325 to 374 answers are correct.

Good: if 375 to 424 answers are correct.

Excellent: if 425 to 475 answers are correct.

And if 476 and above are correct

you are a **SUPER EXPERT** in science!